ANOTHER CAT BOOK

CHARLES ORTLEB
and
ARTHUR HOWARD

ST. MARTIN'S PRESS
NEW YORK

Library of Congress Cataloging in Publication Data

Ortleb, Charles.
  Another cat book.

  1. Cats—Caricatures and cartoons. 2. American wit
and humor, Pictorial. I. Howard, Arthur, joint author.
II. Title.
NC1429.0616A4 1979   741.5'973   79-16396
ISBN 0-312-04195-0

To
Kevin
from
Chuck

Thanks to
Jeremy
and
Didi
from A. H.

"Poems were made
by fools like that,
But only God
can make a cat."

"I'm only going to say it once. I'm in a nail-clipping mood."

"I told you food always tastes better in the country."

"Very existentialist Moo-Moo. Now get down!"

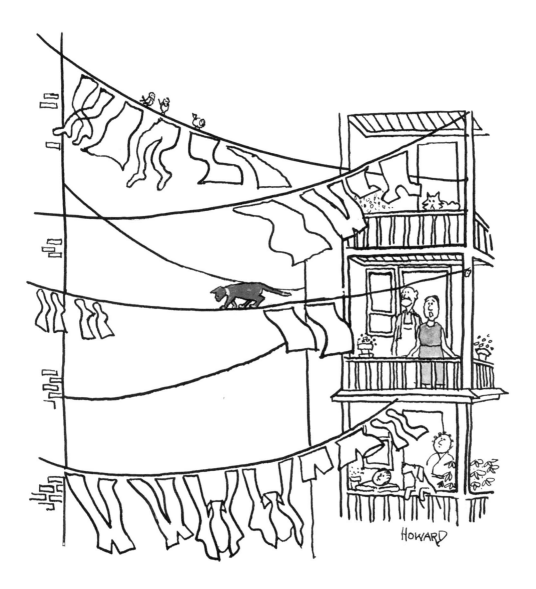

"He's been pacing like that all morning."

HOWARD

"I think he remembers the last time we played veterinarian."

"One more move like that and I'm ordering the piranhas."

"Willamina, sublimate!"

HOWARD

"Quick! Everyone watch TV before the commercial's over!"

"Eat it!"

"Tuna banquet and kidney surprise. Bon appetit!"

"We will eat our sardine on an English, or we will not eat at all."

"Now let us pray for our friends in homes with dogs."

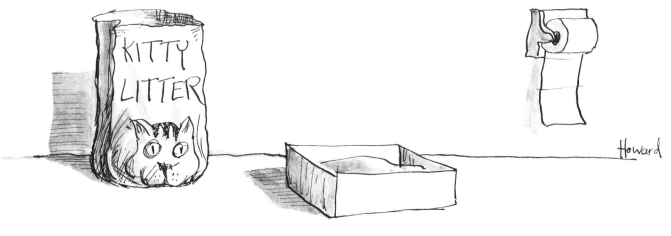

Howard

"No, I said throw me my cap."

"Yes, I see it has great suction."

"Well, I've got your number."

"This is Mrs. Dreiser from the Feline Discipline School. She's here to instill guilt."

"I just want to say a few words to the aggressive ones. I won't identify you by name—you know who you are."

"I think we'd all better T-Group immediately."

"She's been that way ever since she turned six."

"Muffin gets motion sickness."

Cat psychosis.

"Now Taffy, don't ruin this year's Christmas card."

"Happy Birthday to you, Happy Birthday to you . . ."

HOWARD

"So you *can* take it with you!"

"Have you been around cats before?"

"You can take the whiskers off now Rhoda. I've grown to trust you."

"I do hope you like cats."

"There seems to be some interference with one of the speakers."

"Three Capricorns, two Cancers and an Aquarius—and yours?"

"Why is it that we can't find happiness in a recently emptied A & P bag?"

HOWARD

"Oh yes, they're wonderful with children."

"Just what I wanted on my baked potato—you!"

"It's so nice of you to drop in, Mr. Murrow. The children stayed up just to see you."

"I found him in 3G watching old Sonja Henie movies."

During the 1970s the American family experienced a great deal of role reversal.

"Was that you purring or my lasagne?"

"Hope you realize who you're corrupting."

"They're almost human, which is more than I can say for some people around here."

"George has been wonderful ever since I had him declawed."

"Oh, not you too!"

"They sense I'm between marriages."

"I see your friend is into heavy petting."

"How does this sound? 'It was raining. It was really raining. The cat sat by the window purring. The cat was really purring. . . .'"

1979

1980

1981

1982

"Alright, who has the Arts and Leisure section?"

"I assume you'll finish that when you consider all the starving kitties in China."

"If elected, I *will* certainly consider a cat rebate, ma'am."

"You could occasionally step on a cockroach or two."

"I have a full day planned for you. First you'll stare out the window for two hours, then you'll proceed to the bedroom where you'll nuzzle all my slippers until lunch. After lunch you'll move into the living room where you'll swat the 'Do Not Remove Under Penalty of Law' tag under the sofa. And then . . ."

"If Lauren Bacall were here, I bet there wouldn't be so much indifference in this room tonight."

"I'm a V.I.P. and this is my V.I.C."

"Who remembers Frank Sinatra?"

"A penny for your thoughts."

HOWARD

"I make a better real estate agent than scratching post."

"Is there a little real estate in there for me?"

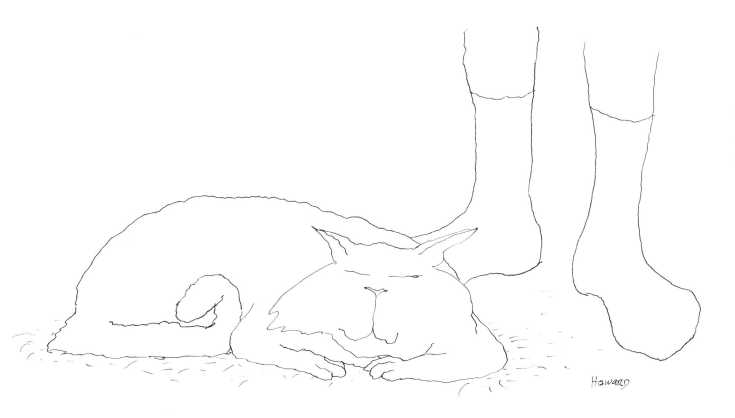

"Do *I* leave hair on *your* toothbrush?"

"Now that's a literary cat. He *loves* the Hamptons."

HOWARD

New types of cats are being bred every day.

A WILDE CAT

The Hirshfield cat.

"Yes, Marmalade's been reading the *New York Review of Books* lately and is unhappy with the stereotypical presentations of his condition like 'The Cat in the Hat Comes Back.'"

"You can take the cat out of L.A., but you can't take the L.A. out of the cat."

HOWARD

"You're very fortunate. I see nine long lives."

"May I recommend the liver with buffalo by-products?"

"I wonder if he lands on all fours."

A Brief History of the Domestic Cat

Cavemen probably liked dogs better . . .

Cavewomen may have preferred cats . . .

In some centuries cats found themselves in an enviable position . . .

"Hail O Glorious One, Daughter of Almighty Ra and the Great Goddess Isis, Giver of Light, Healer of the Sick! Time for din-din."

During the Renaissance the situation for cats improved. Cats figure in many of the non-secular paintings of the period.

But there were times when cat lovers were forced to hide cats.

Eventually cats, like everyone else, were persecuted . . .

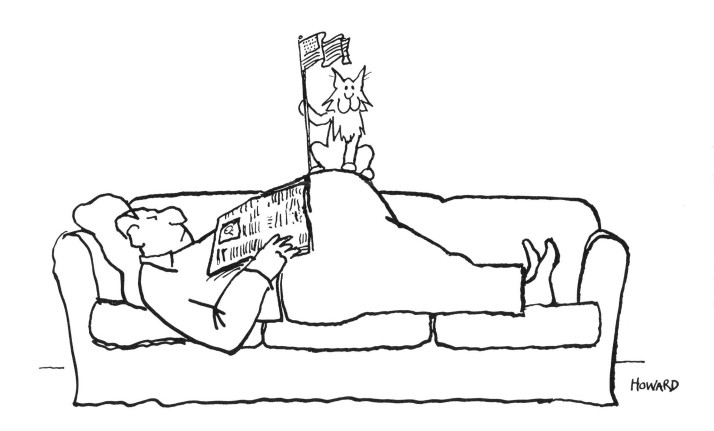

. . . until their final victory in the twentieth century.

A Great Moment in Cat Thought

A Wild Cat Strike

"On the other hand, you are familiar with the concept of the paper tiger."

HOWARD